Abuelita

by Myka-Lynne Sokoloff
illustrated by Johanna van der Sterre

Harcourt
SCHOOL PUBLISHERS

Printed in Mexico

ISBN 10: 0-15-350997-X
ISBN 13: 978-0-15-350997-1

Ordering Options
ISBN 10: 0-15-350602-4 (Grade 5 On-Level Collection)
ISBN 13: 978-0-15-350602-4 (Grade 5 On-Level Collection)
ISBN 10: 0-15-357950-1 (package of 5)
ISBN 13: 978-0-15-357950-9 (package of 5)

2 3 4 5 6 7 8 9 10   126   12 11 10 09 08 07

This story is about me—Esmeralda—and my *abuelita*—
my grandmother. She gave me my name when she first saw
my green eyes. She's the only one who uses my full name.
Everyone else just calls me Emmy. This story is also about
my two favorite things: my little red wagon and the fall. Let
me explain why they are my favorite things.

My little red wagon was a gift from Abuelita and
Abuelito when I was five years old. For the longest time,
I carried everything I owned in that shiny metal vehicle.
I would load my favorite teddy bears, my dolls, my best
friend, or my umbrellas for the sun or rain.
Anything I could make fit went for a
ride in my red wagon.

3

Every afternoon, Abuelita would pick me up from
school. First, we would walk to my house and load some
toys into my red wagon. Then we would wheel them three
doors down to her house. Soon my schoolbooks became
part of the pile, so that I could do my homework at
Abuelita's house. When Mamá or Papá came home from
work, I would load my toys and books back into the wagon
and roll everything home again.

Now that I'm older, I spend most of my time studying
at my grandmother's house after school. Also, now that I
am older, I carry my books in my backpack. This leaves my
little red wagon with little to do. Eventually, my wagon
made its way to the shed behind my house. It doesn't get
much use anymore.

4

I love going to Abuelita's house after school, especially in the fall. In October, as soon as I finish my homework, we get to work on our preparations for *Día de los Muertos*.

Día de los Muertos means "Day of the Dead." The holiday is celebrated during the first two days of November. People go to the cemetery to visit the graves of loved ones. Each year, we load food and decorations into baskets and walk to the cemetery where my grandfather is buried.

In the weeks leading up to this special time of year, we make small skeletons and skulls out of sugar. We also bake sweet bread called *pan de muertos*. The smell of the sweet bread baking in my grandmother's kitchen is irresistible. Sometimes Abuelita also makes *tamales* and a special dish called *mole*. These were my grandfather's favorite foods.

When our kitchen chores are done, we make *papel picado*. We use these colorful paper cutouts to decorate for *Día de los Muertos*. Abuelita is teaching me the old–fashioned way to make them. She uses sharp scissors to make the designs. The decorated papers are used for all kinds of celebrations, especially *Día de los Muertos*.

Some people may think that an event like this is a grim affair. They would really be surprised to come and see all of the revelers at the cemetery. People sing and tell jokes. They eat meals and decorate the graves of their loved ones with paper cutouts and marigolds. Sometimes *mariachi* bands play lively music. We are not celebrating the idea that people we loved have passed away. Instead, we are honoring them and remembering them.

This past October, something terrible happened. My grandmother was leaving the grocery store. Her arms were loaded with items for our holiday preparations. She didn't see the curb and tripped on the sidewalk. Poor Abuelita fell and broke her hip! She had to spend a few weeks in the hospital as it healed. I was afraid there would be no *Día de los Muertos* this year.

Abuelita had other plans. We passed the time at the hospital making *papel picado*. She told me stories about growing up in Mexico. Each time I came to visit, she reminded me, "Esmeralda, I'm depending on you to make the candies for *Día de los Muertos*. Next week, you and your father can bake the *pan de muertos* so that it's fresh."

I felt wistful as I recalled all of those autumns that Abuelita and I had strolled hand in hand to the cemetery. I was relieved that Abuelita would be home from the hospital in time for the holiday. One thing that she neglected to tell me was that she was not supposed to walk for several more weeks.

One day I arrived a few minutes early at the hospital. I heard my grandmother nearly yelling at the doctor! "I am not going to miss planting marigolds on my Hector's grave," she told him.

"Mrs. Rivera, you must promise me that you will not put any weight on that hip," the doctor reminded her sternly.

"We'll just see about that," Abuelita told me in a raspy voice once the doctor left her room.

I knew that Abuelita would be heartbroken to miss the celebration. I knew she had missed my grandfather terribly these past few years. She always seemed happier when she visited his grave. I had to think of some way to help her.

By November, I had a plan. Out in the shed, I unearthed my red wagon. It was pretty dusty but nothing that a good scrubbing couldn't fix.

Abuelita was reluctant about my plan at first. "I am not a kindergartner," she objected. "I will look foolish riding in a child's wagon."

"I'll take care of everything, Abuelita," I promised. "You can count on me."

I found a pretty, old quilt that Abuelita's own mother had made. She would be comfortable sitting on that. I taped marigolds to the wheels of the wagon. Mamá and Papá would carry baskets with breads and sweets, and warm dishes of *tamales* and *mole*. I carefully tucked the *papel picado* under the quilt by Abuelita's knees.

Everyone on our block joined our parade as Mamá, Papá, Abuelita, and I made our way down the street. I had to admit, Abuelita looked very regal as we rolled down the block.

"Mrs. Rivera! Abuelita!" Other neighbors and my cousins swarmed around Abuelita as we rolled into the cemetery. "We never expected to see you this year!"

"Humph!" Abuelita snorted. "What do they think—I'm going to miss this day?"

We decorated my grandfather's grave and had our picnic. Little children chased each other. Everyone sang and laughed. It was a beautiful day, the best ever.

Abuelita was very tired when we finally got back to her house that evening. She looked very happy, though.

"*Mija*," she said, holding my hand. (She often calls me *mija*, short for *mi hija*, which means "my daughter.") "I am so grateful to you for all your help. You did such a wonderful job making the candies, the *pan muertos*, and all the decorations. I could never have come along today if you hadn't thought of using the wagon to carry me!"

"Abuelita," I replied, "I'm so grateful to you, too. Without you, I would never have known how to make *papel picado* or *pan de muertos*. I would never have learned to make *tamales* if you hadn't taught me. I wouldn't even have a red wagon if it weren't for you!"

"We do make a good team, don't we, *mija*?" she said, squeezing my hand.

Think Critically

1. What goal did Esmeralda help Abuelita reach?

2. When did you first think Esmeralda might use the red wagon to solve Abuelita's problem?

3. If you could ask the main characters a question, what would it be?

4. Who is telling this story? How do you know?

5. What meaning did *Día de los Muerto* have for Esmeralda?

Social Studies

Another Holiday Use the Internet or another library resource to research a holiday from another country. Write a short report on the holiday based on what you learn. Be sure to include details about food, decorations, and other traditions.

School-Home Connection Share this book with your family. Together, discuss ideas for something you can do for someone who is special to all of you.

Word Count: 1,195